The Night Before
Christmas

The Night Before Christmas

The Original Story
By Clement C. Moore

Illustrated by James Rice

Pelican Publishing Company
GRETNA 1989

Copyright © 1989
By Pelican Publishing Company, Inc.
All rights reserved

First printing, October 1989
Second printing, December 1989

"An Account of a Visit from St. Nicholas," written by
Clement C. Moore, was first published by the *Sentinel* of
Troy, New York, in 1823.

Library of Congress Cataloging-in-Publication Data

Moore, Clement Clarke, 1779-1863.
      The night before Christmas / by Clement C. Moore ;
illustrated by James Rice.
          p.   cm.
      Summary: Saint Nicholas visits a sleeping household on
Christmas Eve.
      ISBN 0-88289-755-1
      1. Santa Claus--Juvenile poetry. 2. Christmas--Juvenile
poetry. 3. Children's poetry, American.   [1. Santa Claus--Poetry.
2. Christmas--Poetry. 3. Narrative poetry. 4. American poetry.]
I. Rice, James, 1934-   ill. II. Title.
PS2429.M5N5 1989d
811'.2--dc20   89-34789
                                                                CIP
                                                                AC
Manufactured in Hong Kong
Published by Pelican Publishing Company, Inc.
1101 Monroe Street, Gretna, Louisiana 70053

I was the night before Christmas,
when all through the house
Not a creature was stirring,
not even a mouse.

he stockings were hung
by the chimney with care,
In hopes that St. Nicholas
soon would be there.

The children were nestled
all snug in their beds,
While visions of sugarplums
danced in their heads.

nd mamma in her 'kerchief,
and I in my cap,
Had just settled our brains
for a long winter's nap . . .

When out on the lawn
    there arose such a clatter,
I sprang from the bed
    to see what was the matter.

way to the window
I flew like a flash,
Tore open the shutters
and threw up the sash.

The moon on the breast
   of the new-fallen snow
Gave the lustre of mid-day
   to objects below,

hen, what to my wondering
eyes should appear,
But a miniature sleigh,
and eight tiny reindeer,

With a little old driver,
   so lively and quick,
I knew in a moment
   it must be St. Nick.

ore rapid than eagles
his coursers they came,
And he whistled, and shouted,
and called them by name:

"Now, Dasher! now, Dancer!
  now, Prancer and Vixen!
On, Comet! on, Cupid!
  on, Donner and Blitzen!

o the top of the porch!
    to the top of the wall!
Now dash away! dash away!
    dash away all!"

As dry leaves that before
    the wild hurricane fly,
When they meet with an obstacle,
    mount to the sky,

So up to the house-top
    the coursers they flew,
With the sleigh full of toys,
    and St. Nicholas too.

nd then, in a twinkling,
I heard on the roof
The prancing and pawing
of each little hoof.

As I drew in my head,
　　and was turning around,
Down the chimney St. Nicholas came
　　with a bound.

e was dressed all in fur,
from his head to his foot,

And his clothes were all tarnished
with ashes and soot.

bundle of toys he had flung
on his back,
And he looked like a peddler
just opening his pack.

His eyes—how they twinkled
    —his dimples how merry!
His cheeks were like roses,
    his nose like a cherry!

His droll little mouth
          was drawn up like a bow,
And the beard of his chin
          was as white as the snow.

The stump of a pipe he held
   tight in his teeth,
And the smoke it encircled
   his head like a wreath.

e had a broad face
and a little round belly
That shook, when he laughed,
like a bowl full of jelly.

He was chubby and plump,
    a right jolly old elf,
And I laughed when I saw him,
    in spite of myself.

wink of his eye
and a twist of his head
Soon gave me to know
I had nothing to dread.

He spoke not a word,
  but went straight to his work,
And filled all the stockings;
  then turned with a jerk,

nd laying his finger
aside of his nose,
And giving a nod,
up the chimney he rose.

He sprang to his sleigh,
    to his team gave a whistle,
And away they all flew
    like the down of a thistle.

But I heard him exclaim,
   ere he drove out of sight,
"Happy Christmas to all,
   and to all a good-night!"